Truth Be Told

by Lisa Soland

A SAMUEL FRENCH ACTING EDITION

SAMUEL FRENCH

FOUNDED 1830

NEW YORK HOLLYWOOD LONDON TORONTO

SAMUELFRENCH.COM

IMPORTANT BILLING AND CREDIT REQUIREMENTS

All producers of *TRUTH BE TOLD must* give credit to the Author of the Play in all programs distributed in connection with performances of the Play, and in all instances in which the title of the Play appears for the purposes of advertising, publicizing or otherwise exploiting the Play and/or a production. The name of the Author *must* appear on a separate line on which no other name appears, immediately following the title and *must* appear in size of type not less than fifty percent of the size of the title type.

TRUTH BE TOLD was originally produced at The Actor's Group in North Hollywood, California, on June 22, 2008. It was directed by Lisa Soland, produced by Rose's Name Game Productions and the production stage manager was Vincent Archer. The cast, in order of appearance, was as follows:

THE SHOE FETISH . . . . Jeri Zucchi
THE KIND THAT DOESN'T BUDGE . . . . Todd Covert
THE EYES OF A MOTHER . . . . Melanie Ewbank
PLAIDS AND STRIPES . . . . Jeremy Juuso
THE QUILT MAKER. . . . . Susan C. Hunter
THE DENTAL HYGIENIST . . . . David Purdham
SHUFFLEBOARD . . . . Bill Lewis
SENSITIVITY. . . . . Michelle DeLynn
IT'S THE SIMPLE THINGS . . . . Chris Durmick
THE FREEWHEELIN' BOB DYLAN . . . . Joe McClain
CAUGHT IN A LIE . . . . Miranda Kent

The monologue "The Kind that Doesn't Budge" was first produced on July 27, 2006, for the Short Attention Span PlayFEST by Atlantis Playmakers in Lowell, Massachusetts. The piece was performed by Michael Molineaux and directed by Amy Joy Laffin.

CHARACTERS

JERI: Between twenty-five and forty.
TODD: Late twenties to forties.
MELANIE: A woman of any age.
JEREMY: Between the ages of thirty and forty.
ANN: Between sixty and eighty years old.
DAVID: A fifty-four year old, blue collar worker.
BILL: Between the ages of thirty and forty-five.
MICHELLE: Thirties.
CHRIS: Forties.
JOEY: Late fifties, visibly disabled.
MIRANDA: A married woman of any age.

PLACE

A bare stage.

TIME

The present.

PRODUCTION NOTES

Truth Be Told is a full-length play to be performed without intermission. The order of the pieces works. Trust it. Each monologue has its own voice, style and personality, so the pace of each should vary according to those individual personalities. Actors should take care to avoid becoming inwardly focused. Monologues are best delivered as selflessly and as generously as if one were playing them with a scene partner. For the actor, being part of this production can be an exercise in simple storytelling, which is not too often simple. It's about the story. Keep the sustained intent on telling the story.

A SPECIAL ACKNOWLEDGMENT

Over my career I have been richly blessed to work alongside some very talented people, particularly actors. Most of the actors who originated the roles in *Truth Be Told*, I've worked with and have known for a very long time. Chris Durmick and I were two of twenty students accepted into Florida State University's BFA acting program. While there, I had the pleasure of watching him, one of my favorite physical comedians, perform a brilliant *Scapino*. Jeri Zucchi and I were two of twelve apprentices who spent a year at the Burt Reynolds Jupiter Theatre, working hard in order to earn our Actors' Equity memberships. Our master teacher, Charles Nelson Reilly, directed us in William Luce's world premiere of *Luce Women* – Jeri portrayed Emily Dickinson alongside my Zelda Fitzgerald.

While performing in a critically acclaimed production of *Grease*, I met and became friends with the multi-talented Bill Lewis. Melanie Ewbank and I met while doing a production of Agatha Christie's *Black Coffee*. Joe McClain and Miranda Kent premiered roles in my comedy *Waiting* and Jeremy Juuso in my drama *The ReBirth*. And Todd Covert and I met when he was cast to play Simon Peter in the Southern California tour of my play, *The Lord's Last Supper.*

The reason I've worked with these people over and over again is not only because they're massively talented – that goes without saying – but because they are self-reliant, hard working, reliable craftsmen. Craftsmen. They come in prepared and they knock your socks off. Period.

I dedicate this play to them and those of you like them – creative souls passionate about helping develop and shape new plays. The theatre cannot exist without you. And with you, it's magical.

L.S.
Los Angeles, July 2009

Contents

The Shoe Fetish 9

The Kind That Doesn't Budge 15

The Eyes of a Mother 19

Plaids and Stripes. 23

The Quilt Maker 27

The Dental Hygienist. 33

Shuffleboard. 35

Sensitivity 39

It's the Simple Things 43

The Freewheelin' Bob Dylan 47

Caught in a Lie 51

THE SHOE FETISH

*(**AT RISE:** Lights come up on **JERI**, a pleasant woman between the ages of 25 and 40. The stage is bare but for a shoe organizer containing twelve pairs of shoes, hanging stage left. She addresses the audience.)*

JERI. Last week I went to DSW. You know, that discount shoe place by the mall? They were having some kind of amazing sale, like fifty percent off stuff that had already been marked down fifty percent.

(beat)

Wait. That can't be right.

(beat)

Anyway, I think, "How can I go wrong?" Right?

(beat)

I spot these black pumps with a low heel. Now I know I've already got two pairs of black pumps at home but these, oh but these… These are the kind I *really* wanted, with the perfect level heel and the slightly squared toe. And the best part was I got them for only ten bucks. Ten bucks! And they're leather, not that cheap crap. An excellent buy, what can I say.

(beat)

I get home and there's this message from my brother saying that he's got this great guy he wants me to meet. He gives me his number, I call him and we decide to meet for dinner. And my first thought was, "Ah huh! This must be meant to be – new shoes, blind date. New shoes, blind date."

(beat)

JERI. *(cont.)* Now here's where you got to be careful. Wearing the new shoes out of the house. If you wear them *inside* the house, you're okay...

(She removes one shoe to show the audience what she means.)

The wear on the bottom doesn't show and you can still return them. But once you walk out that front door, THAT'S IT. You're fully committed to your purchase. Scares the heck out of me, fully committed.

(beat)

But on the other hand, I'm thinking this must be some sort of sign, you know? – buying a new pair of shoes on the same night that I'm going out with a new guy. So I open the door and walk right out.

(beat)

We meet for dinner, hit if off, decide to stay in each other's company a bit longer. We walk over to the coffee shop and continue to hit it off – so much in common. I can't believe it. Then we walk over to the bookstore and by now I'm starting to notice that these shoes aren't at all what they first seemed to be. They're beginning to disappoint me, greatly.

(disappointed)

I mean, ten bucks, right? You get what you pay for. How many times do I have to learn *that* one?!

(beat)

Since my right foot is slightly larger then my left, I'm starting to feel the pain there first and begin to limp profusely, on the right side. Let me tell you something – limping is not good on a date, especially a blind date because they have nothing to compare the limping to. They can't refer back to all the other times they saw you when you *didn't* limp. They just immediately start thinking you're an old gray mare who needs to be taken out to pasture and shot. Hey, I'm not exaggerating. They do that in Kentucky. I'm from there and I know.

(beat)

JERI. *(cont.)* I start projecting my insecurities all over this guy, however great I thought he was, and imagine that he would never marry a girl with a limp so I'm trying desperately to walk straight...

(She crosses stage right, trying to walk without a limp.)

...you know – level. Impossible. This black leather shoe, supposedly from Italy, is now causing my right leg to go numb. Numb from the hip down. Numb is not good on a blind date.

(beat)

We're almost to the Barnes and Noble and he stops and turns to me and says...

(imitating him)

"Hey, what's with the limp?" And I'm thinking, "Oh, my God. It wasn't my imagination. These stupid new shoes are going to end the best date of my life." But because I'm really liking this guy, I patiently say to him, "It's these shoes. I just bought them today and they're too tight."

(imitating him)

"Oh, you got that *shoe fetish* thing going on. My last girlfriend had that and she emptied out my entire checking account."

(beat)

"Oh, no, no. That's not me. I only go for the buys."

(imitating him)

JERI. *(cont.)* "Oh, really? What kind of great discount did you get on these shoes that make you limp?"

(beat)

Now it was perfectly clear that he was judging me all over the place and to tell you the truth, I had had it with the dating game of presenting some sort of false self until you can't stand it any longer and then you finally let down your hair. So, right then and there I decided I wasn't going to do that anymore. I was going to make a commitment – a commitment to myself to tell the truth about who I am. To put it all out there. Come hell or high water, I was going to be me, damn it.

(She addresses him.)

"Listen," I said. "I'm not perfect, by any means. In fact, making the wrong choice on these shoes is only *one* of the *many* mistakes I've made in my life. And if you are the kind of person who has only one pair of brown shoes and one pair of black shoes in your closet then yes, I guess you could say that I have one major shoe fetish. In fact, hanging over not just one, but every door in my apartment is a shoe organizer which contains exactly twelve pairs of shoes each. One has brown shoes, one has black, one has beige and one is for summer, mostly sandals. Oh, and the one hanging over the bathroom door contains boots of various textures and shades. Now I know that there are some guys who would be threatened by that. Not by the shoes, but threatened by the fact that I'm not perfect. But I can promise you this – I will not empty your bank account. That is, unless you let me. Just kidding. A relationship takes two. Me *and* you. Not just me. It takes communication and it takes some risks. I've had such a lovely time with you tonight. If you're willing to continue this process of getting to know each other, well then, I am too."

(beat)

He looks at me and I notice that he's not all anxious looking, you know – thinking I'm weird or too bold or something. And then he says, "Okay." Just like that, "Okay." We decide to skip the bookstore and go to my house for dessert but all he really seems interested in is my collection of…120 or so odd pairs of shoes.

(beat)

JERI. *(cont.)* He sits back on my sofa and makes me try on every, single pair – you know, model them for him in the living room.

(She models the shoes as if on a runway.)

I felt like I was on a runway or something. He'd ask, "Now, how do those feel? Be honest now." And I'd say, "They feel tight." And then we'd add them to the pile. By six in the morning every pair of shoes that didn't fit right or I didn't really like were in a pile by my front door…

*(**JERI** crosses stage left.)*

…but these.

(She refers to the shoe organizer.)

These are what we ended up with – twelve pairs of shoes. And none of them hurt me. Simple, really. I brought the others into work and the women went nuts. Well, the ones with the small feet did, 'cause a lot of these shoes were brand new, just too small or too… something or other.

(beat)

A hundred, some odd pairs, now gone. I don't even miss them! I miss him, though. But I won't have to miss him for long. We're going to the beach tomorrow, 'cause he says I have the most beautiful feet and he wants to look at them all day long!

(blackout)

THE KIND THAT DOESN'T BUDGE

TODD. No, no. It's not the commitment thing. Come on, man. You know me. I'm committed in a lot of areas of my life. It's not that. It's just well…

(hesitant)

When I was in second grade I had this teacher – Mrs. Moore. I didn't have a crush on her or anything. It wasn't like that. She was just…amazing.

(beat)

She was plain but smart. Man, she never forgot a thing. And we all wanted to please her for some reason. Just make her happy somehow.

(beat)

She had this long, black hair. Beautiful, shiny, sort of bluish, you know? – when the light hit it just right. And she always wore it up, in a tight bun. Always. Every day. This perfect, round bun, neatly gathered above her neck.

(beat)

TODD. *(cont.)* Mrs. Moore had a son, Danny, and he was in the second grade too but he couldn't be in her class with me, because he was her son, so he was in the other second grade. He was my buddy and we would go to each other's houses a lot, you know – hang out. Play, I guess.

(beat)

TODD. *(cont.)* One time I was over there and we were getting ready for bed, brushing our teeth and I walk down the hall to the bathroom and pass by his mother's room. The door was open. It was just a quick look, you know – a glance, but I saw her sitting at this table with a mirror in front of her and she had her hair, her beautiful hair down, brushing it with one of those, you know, those old fashioned brushes with the ivory handles. She was wearing a robe, a blue robe and her hair fell all the way down to her waist.

(thinking back)

Brushing. Just brushing.

(pause)

I was speechless. Couldn't talk for days. For days. My mom took me to the doctor. They thought something was wrong with me.

(shakes his head)

For days.

(beat)

Well, a couple of months ago I went back for my high school reunion and got together with Danny. Hadn't seen him since…graduation. He couldn't go to the reunion. He was back living with his mother in that same house. His dad had passed away a while ago and his mom, my second grade teacher had Alzheimer's. Has Alzheimer's. Danny has to keep the doors locked and stuff 'cause she forgets where she is and runs out, all the time. Just runs out. I noticed all the padlocks are up high, out of reach. And he's got to make sure they're always locked.

(beat)

She didn't remember me. I guess something inside of me hoped she would. But she didn't. And her long, black hair was still long but gray – kinky, worn, and pulled into some sort of tangled mess in the back. It looked like it hadn't been brushed in weeks. But still long. I sat there at the kitchen table and watched them, the two of them, fight down her lunch. She wouldn't eat. Danny had fixed her a sandwich – two slices of plain bread with a chunk of cheese in the middle and he tried to…force her, really… He tried to force her to eat it. But she sat there and kept spitting it back up. She'd push it out with her tongue and say things that didn't make any sense. Truthfully? It was pretty tough to watch, me, an outsider, but Danny sat there. He sat there getting food spit all over him and he didn't budge. He didn't budge.

(beat)

It's not that I want a woman like that, with long hair or anything. I just remember that kind of…commitment. That kind of love. The kind that doesn't budge. That's what I want. That's what I'm waiting for.

(blackout)

THE EYES OF A MOTHER

(AT RISE: **MELANIE,** *a woman of any age, stands at a small table, chopping cabbage. After a few moments, she addresses the audience.)*

MELANIE. When I was a kid, I used to have these panic attacks about death. Panic attacks that were…terrifying, really. They would hit me in specific locations, like in bed, before I would fall asleep and in the bathtub. I would be lying there, immersed in the water, and then suddenly it would strike and I would jump out of the tub and start shaking my hands, hard and fast, trying desperately to stop the thoughts that were causing me total anxiety.

(reiterating)

Panic attacks. About death. And I was a kid, young.

(beat)

After one particularly frightening episode, I took a chance and decided to mention it to my older brother, Sam. I thought he might be able to offer me some sort of solace, you know, him being older and everything. I don't remember his response. I think it was something like, "Ah, don't worry about it." But a couple days later, the family was gathered around the dinner table eating, and my mother looks at me in front of everyone and says, "So I understand you're having panic attacks about dying? Is this true?"

(beat)

And I noticed there was this…*spirit* in her eyes, a spirit that a kid not only doesn't want to see, but certainly doesn't want to admit to herself exists in the eyes of her mother – her disposition, the manner in which she changed the way she sat in the chair. You know, pulling one leg up underneath her like the conversation just got interesting or something.

(beat)

MELANIE. *(cont.)* I didn't know what to say. I was expected to say something to defend myself. I knew right away that Sam had gone to her and told her what I had shared with him in secret. And then there was this feeling that *everyone* knew – my other siblings, my dad, the neighbors…the President of the United States. Everyone!

(beat)

And then the cloud rolled in. The great, big, black cloud of doubt rolled right in and I sat soaked in humiliation. "What an idiot I am for thinking such thoughts! How stupid can a kid be? Only older people, people who are near death's door, people who are smarter than me, deep thinkers, people of aristocracy, HAMLET, only *they* should be thinking such thoughts of death and grave despair. Not a young girl of seven with three hamsters and a stamp collection under her bed. Not me. What's wrong with *me*!"

(pause)

Silence filled the room.

(trying to find the right words)

It was as if death itself had crawled beneath the front door and made its way into our home. I glanced around the table at these…strangers, and somehow knew not to speak.

(sarcastically)

After all, I was from another planet. They'd never understand anyway.

(beat)

Then came the laughter. Giggles at first, then the roar. The roar – something I liked to be a part of when I wasn't the subject.

(pause)

MELANIE. *(cont.)* The one containing the most dysfunction runs the family and so she spoke, as only the true matriarch can speak, "You're too young to be worrying about such things. Pass the cabbage."

(with poignancy)

Pass the cabbage.

(beat)

It wasn't until later in my life, when I had formed relationships with people who were "from other planets" too, that the panic attacks eventually subsided. But they did eventually subside. I wasn't alone, although I was led to believe I was.

(blackout)

PLAIDS AND STRIPES

(AT RISE: **JEREMY**, *a man between the ages of 30 and 40, is wearing badly, mismatched clothes – plaids and stripes. He stands center stage, smiling, as he lets the audience make up their mind about him and then begins to talk.)*

JEREMY. I know. You're all looking at me, criticizing me because I don't match. And I want you to know that I'm okay with that.

(beat)

Because what you *don't* know is that I dress like this on purpose. I wear combinations like this because it... sets me free. People look at me, make up their minds about me and then leave me alone. No more staring, no more studying – freedom. I'm free.

(beat)

You know that feeling you get when you walk into a room full of people and everyone kind of "pays you mind?" Like the post office. I used to walk in there wearing my Georgio Armani suit and Bruno Magli shoes...

(an aside to audience, referring to his outfit)

I know, it's hard to believe that now...

(continuing)

...but I would go in there to buy rolls of stamps for my office and it was unbearable – the feeling I would get. Very hard on the stomach. Ulcers. I got ulcers from dressing like that. Everyone would look and I could feel them wondering, "Who the hell does he think *he* is?" You know, wondering where I got my money and thinking that I would do something stupid in the very near future and lose it all – the house, the boat, the stock options, the whole sha-bang. They treated me, without knowing me at all, like I was…a jerk.

(beat)

JEREMY. *(cont.)* I walk in there now, with a bit of a wardrobe change, and people look, judge and write me off all within about thirty seconds and then I can stand there peacefully and not be bothered by the faultfinders of the world. It's like my very own screening process.

(beat)

People that are worth their weight in gold? – they talk to me when no one else does. They figure, "Hey, if nothing else, the guy's interesting." That's how I met my wife.

(beat)

I was wearing my favorite that day – plaids and stripes. But not *gentle* colors. Uh, ah. Something loud, vibrant. It was in the bank. You know – the usual long line – eight windows, two tellers, that sort of thing. A stunning woman with long blonde hair standing behind me, said something about how everyone must have gone to lunch, which didn't make sense to her, seeing that everyone who worked in the area came to use the bank on their lunch hour. See? Smart. Worth her weight in gold. I said to her that I agreed. And off we were talking away. She asked why I wore the clothes I did and I told her. I told her the truth, which was probably new to someone this pretty and we were married six months later.

(smiling)

You should have seen what we wore for the wedding. I won't go into it but it was *spectacular.* Even the photographer left us alone. There were much more attractive things to photograph, like the flowers, the cake…the floor.

(He chuckles.)

JEREMY. *(cont.)* So we got to enjoy ourselves over in a corner somewhere. You know, talking about what we were going to do with the rest of our lives.

(beat)

These movie stars. I don't know how they do it. Under the lens all the time. Under the *gun,* is more like it. People like to see these sorts of people fail. That's just the way it is. But once they figure out you're a nobody, they leave you alone.

(proudly)

Both my wife and I have *the most...*thought provoking, stimulating, curiously odd wardrobe known to man, *and* the greatest friends the world has ever known. I've never been more happy and fulfilled in my entire life.

(blackout)

THE QUILT MAKER

(AT RISE: **ANN**, *a woman between 60 and 80 years of age, is sitting in a chair with a homemade quilt laid out over her lap.)*

ANN. *(cheerfully)* This is what I do. This is what I was born to do. I could do it all day. I often do. The clock may do what it does but I pay no mind. I sew. It's a blessing to find what one was born to do. Many don't. Many people wander around, stumbling into things, but I knew straight off. My mother taught me and her mother taught her and I like to think of it as something we can pass down through the generations, but…

(shrugs)

Well…sometimes it doesn't work out that way.

(beat)

I do some canning in the summer but since the winters are longer, I do this more; to help keep people warm. And they do. Better than most things.

(looking down at her quilt)

Keep people warm.

(beat)

This is a replica of my first quilt. I made it for my daughter. It's what they call a sampler quilt because each square has a different pattern. I learned in a class taught by my mother, so she could make some extra money, but I got to take the class for free. I was the only one who finished. She would give us three new patterns a week, to work on at home, and I did what she asked of me. That's why I finished. I put them together, sewed them up and brought them back to class the next week. I never understood why the others didn't do the same – do what they were told. This is the way you learn. This is the way you get things done.

(beat)

ANN. *(cont.)* Today someone making a quilt will just go out and buy the fabric, because there's money around today but back then, back when *I* started sewing, you used the scraps – the scraps from other things you'd made along the way – pieces of material that might otherwise be wasted. See? See this material here? This is from my daughter's eighth grade graduation dress. I made it for her. Ladies were wearing those floor-length dresses back then and I put white lace around the sleeves and the collar. It was lovely. She didn't like it. She said it itched her neck. But I got her to agree to this pattern and fabric because I promised to make her a shirt with horses all over it. She loved *that* material. Let's see…

(She looks for that material in the quilt.)

I guess I didn't use that horse print in this quilt, because… Well, truth be told, I didn't like it. But she did. She loved horses. Loved them.

(beat)

When she was a very little girl, my mother made her a baby quilt and she loved that quilt. Just loved it. Carried it with her wherever she went. One day I finally took it away from her because all that was left was one, paper thin square.

(She squares it out on the quilt.)

Can you imagine? She cried and she cried. Always wanted me to make her another "blankie" but I… Well, I never got around to it…till afterwards. So much to do.

(beat)

ANN. *(cont.)* We bought her a horse, when young girls yearn for that sort of thing, and then she wanted me to make her a blanket for the horse, cried and cried, but… Well, too much work goes into them, these quilts, and I just couldn't see her throwing it over the sweaty back of a horse and slamming a saddle down on top of it. I tried to explain but…

(She shakes her head.)

Well, she was crazy about horses.

(She touches the quilt.)

I like the Grandmother's Fan pattern. It's very pretty. It looks like a fan.

(She spreads out her fingers like a fan.)

It fans out and it has strips of different material in it. But each block is the same. Each fan is the same color. It's hard to make that one from scraps because you need so much of the same fabric. I found a Grandmother's Fan quilt in my mother's farm house after she passed away and it had worn itself so thin you could see right clear to the lining – the batting, and I discovered that my mother had sewn an old winter coat… she had used an old winter coat and sewn it in as part of the lining of the quilt. Can you believe it? But you see that's what you did back then. You used everything you had. No one had any money so that's what you did. These quilts were made out of necessity back then, to keep warm, and that's what you used them for. The farm house was cold, not much heat, because the heat came from wood and sometimes you ran out of wood so you'd sit in the house with a quilt thrown over your legs, just to keep warm. Winters were very cold.

(looking down at quilt draped over her legs)

ANN. *(cont.)* This is what I do, now. Drape it over my legs. 'Cause I get cold, guess 'cause I'm old. Old people get cold. Plenty of heat now, just old. I still love to sew. I could do it all day. The clock does what it does but I pay no mind, I sew. It's a blessing. Many people wander around not knowing what it is they want to do with their lives. But we need to do what we think will make us happy, and then when we learn better, we can adjust, but life's too short. It was too short for my daughter.

(She looks down at the quilt.)

ANN. *(cont.)* See, this pattern goes like this – a mirror image here and then it repeats, over and over and over again. It makes sense, right? But life isn't like that. Life sometimes has no pattern and it doesn't make any sense at all. They call that a crazy quilt. Yes. Yes, they do. A crazy quilt, and it can go any which way. No rhyme or reason. It's a great quilt to make because it can use up all those little scraps you might have in your sewing box. It puts every little scrap to use. And that's the way life is sometimes – it's just plain crazy. But you have to use the scraps you've got, the scraps that the good Lord gives you, and put them to some use. Show that there's some value in it even when it's crazy.

(beat)

See this material here? This calico? This was from her wedding dress. No one wears calico on their wedding day, but she did. I tried to talk her out of it but... Well, she had her own mind and she used it. Calico. They sped off on their honeymoon, with the cans tied to the bumper, banging about. Her husband was driving. It was Memorial Day weekend and I guess the freeway traffic was terrible. He got off the main road to... I guess so he could drive faster and didn't see the stop sign, and a semi hit them, broadside. Didn't see the stop sign. See, the stop sign, if he'd seen it, well, that's why signs are there. We obey them and they keep us safe. *If* we see them. She died instantly. Instantly. No children.

(beat)

It's hard for a mother, a parent, to watch her little girl…pass on…before *you* do, because it just doesn't make sense. It's not the normal order of things. Crazy.

(beat)

So every Memorial Day I pull out this quilt. This quilt she never got a chance to see. To use. It's a tradition I would have liked to have carried down through the generations but I guess it's enough to just, rest it here on my lap and…keep me warm.

(blackout)

THE DENTAL HYGIENIST

*(**AT RISE:** **DAVID**, a fifty-four year old, blue collar worker [perhaps a mechanic], is sitting with a small table to his left. On the table sits a bowl and a Dixie cup containing Listerine. He has a paper towel clipped around his neck and he addresses Sally who stands above him.)*

DAVID. I'm fifty-four years old and I've been coming in here, to this dentist, a very long time and just because you tell me now that I'm not brushing properly does not mean that I'm going to rush home and start brushing correctly.

(He rinses his mouth out with Listerine and spits into the bowl.)

You have to understand that for years I've been going to the dentist and the dental hygienist, as they now call you. You used to be called *teeth cleaners*. People like you have been telling me that I must floss every day for years, so I go home and I floss every day but after a couple of months of diligently flossing every day, I start to forget and not care, really. I eventually drop down to every other day, then every third day. Then when I come back in here, six months later, sometimes one year later (whether you like it or not), when I come back in here, you ask me if I've been flossing every day and I say, "No." Mainly because I tell the truth. I'm an honest guy. What do you know about that? There're still some of us around, although no one ever seems to acknowledge it. No one I know, anyway.

(beat)

Would you like for me to lie? Is that what you'd like? I know what I'm like. I know what I do and this is what I do. I'm fifty-four.

(beat)

DAVID. *(cont.)* I can try harder, I really can. I can go home now and really try to floss every day but I'm old enough to know that after a couple of months I'll start to fail once more, dropping down to every other day at first, and then every third day or just whenever I have red meat 'cause as you get older, and I am getting older whether I like it or not, as you get older larger spaces begin to form between your teeth and it's a trap for red meat, which I love to eat regardless of what my cardiologist says. A lot of other things start to happen too when one ages, which I won't go into 'cause no one wants to talk about that, especially not you – an aging *woman.*

(He removes the paper towel from around his neck and places it on the table.)

Now, Sally, we can keep playing this game we play, with me coming in here and trying to be the obedient patient, and not lying, and making you really mad, or you can come home with me and make sure I floss every single day of the rest of my life by marrying me like I've been asking you to do every time I come in here.

(beat)

Come home with me and make sure I floss…and I'll make sure you change your oil. Now we aren't getting any younger and another six months can really matter at our age.

(beat)

DAVID. *(cont.)* When was the last time you had your oil changed? You're supposed to change your oil every 3,000 miles. Sometimes I forget to floss my teeth, but I always remember to change my oil. So…

(beat)

What do you say?

(blackout)

SHUFFLEBOARD

(AT RISE: **BILL,** *a man between the ages of 30 and 45, stands center stage and addresses his wife, who has just shared with him that she wants to quit her job and stay at home with their two boys.)*

BILL. *(nodding his head)* Then that's what we're going to do. We're going to figure out what we need to do so you can stay home.

(beat)

I mean, look at this place. This house is twenty-four hundred square feet. We don't need this much space. We've got two kids, not twelve. And they're boys. They can share a room, for God's sake. It'll be good for them. We'll get them bunk beds and they'll learn how to get along in tighter quarters. We can do this, Sheila. We're just going to have to down size and get rid of a lot of this junk we've collected over the past however many years.

(beat)

You and I have three winter coats each. Do you realize that?

(He crosses to closet stage right and pulls out, one at a time, his three winter coats, still on the hangers, and tosses them center stage.)

Three winter coats each? What do we need with three winter coats?

(sarcastic)

Oh, I know – we need one for skiing, one for shoveling the snow and then we need the nice leather coats, that don't really keep us warm, for what? For what?! For church?! What are we afraid of? Are we afraid that if we wore our "shoveling snow" coat to church that no one would talk to us? I'm tired of going to church cold. Let's get rid of the damn things.

(He crosses towards her, now standing with the coats at his feet.)

BILL. *(cont.)* You know what we've done, Sheila? You know the strange truth? We've given away quality time with each other, you and me, with the boys, just so we could own three different winter coats, when all we ever needed was one – the warm one.

(He picks up the warm coat and puts it on.)

A couple of years before we met, I drove back to Osh Gosh to see the first house I lived in as a kid. Just for the fun of it. I knocked on the door and the current owners were home. I told them who I was and that my family had lived in this house about thirty years ago. They asked if I would like to come in and walk around, maybe I would remember something about the place. What I did not remember was that the house was so, so very small. Tiny. I went from room to room and I could not figure out for the life of me, where my parents put us all. Six kids! We must have shared rooms, two or three per room, because there were only…uh, one, two, three bedrooms upstairs and downstairs off the main recreation room, there was this dinky room about 8 feet by 8 feet where I think they put my brother and me. Funny thing is, I don't remember ever feeling crowded.

(beat)

But what I did remember was the tile in the basement floor. My dad put these special tiles in the floor of the basement for shuffleboard. You know? The game where you push the puck down towards these num-bered squares?

(He imitates the motion.)

BILL. *(cont.)* My dad had laid tiles right in the floor. And you know, thirty years later, they were still there. We pulled back the carpet and there they were, black and white and red pieces of tile. The owners didn't know what they were for so they just covered them up with carpet. I explained to them that it was for shuffleboard and they didn't even know what shuffleboard was. They had no idea.

(beat)

The moment I laid my eyes on that tile, the memories of all the fun we had in that basement just came flooding right back in. That's what I remember, Sheila – the fun.

(He takes off the coat and hangs it back in the closet, leaving the others.)

I want our children to have fun. I don't want them shuffled from here to there, to preschool, to the babysitter. If you're feeling like you want to stay home with them, those two beautiful boys, well, I think that's great.

(After a beat, he kicks the two coats still lying on the stage.)

(blackout)

SENSITIVITY

*(AT RISE: **MICHELLE**, a pretty woman in a pretty dress, between the ages of 30 and 40, sits on a stool and addresses the audience.)*

MICHELLE. I've always had this…sensitivity. It's a…sensitivity. I don't know how else to describe it. Looking back now, I think it's because I wasn't happy with life. That life somehow was something to be avoided, you know, the way it was. Reality was to be avoided.

(beat)

When I was a kid, I could pretty much feel what other people were feeling. I could feel it so strongly that my own feelings, what *I* was feeling, was pretty much put on the back burner. And it continued that way until I eventually wound up becoming somebody I really wasn't. And after two disastrous, long term relationships, I decided that I was going to face whatever it was that was keeping me from…living out the life that *I* was supposed to live.

(beat)

I found this therapist and he was good. Really good. I got lucky. A lot of people don't. And he sat there quiet… mostly, for about two years. You know, a lot of people aren't quiet when you talk and quiet is good. Quiet helps. That alone, pretty much got me back on track.

(beat)

But anyway, during this time I gathered up the courage to sign up with this online dating service. I was traveling so much with my work that I thought this would be a good way to meet people – to get out. I tried not to set the parameters too narrow, you know? Filling out those questionnaires? I think I put something like thirty to forty years old and they set me up with this guy, thirty, I guess, and we met for coffee. That's what you do. You meet for coffee and decide whether or not you want to continue the date from there. Well, we did. Everything was okay, so we walked across the street to this Mexican restaurant to grab a bite to eat. It was nice. We had a nice time. And when we walked back to our cars, I remember standing by his SUV and thinking to myself, that he wanted to kiss me. I could feel it. So I just waited around, you know, kind of trying to give him an opportunity, but he didn't. So after a few more minutes we said goodbye and I went home. When I walked in the door, there's this email waiting for me from him, saying how he had wanted to kiss me. And I wrote him back and said, "Well…you should have!"

(beat)

MICHELLE. *(cont.)* Anyway, it was cute. Nothing big or anything. Just kind of simple. I suppose I mostly pursued it because I was lonely. I was pretty much…really lonely. So a couple of days later, I'm given this assignment at work with this impossible deadline. And I'm only able to sleep about two hours a night and then I'm up again, working. Well, I'm on the computer and it's Saturday morning and this guy instant messages me. Says he wants to *see me* and I'm thinking, "This isn't a good time," you know? Also, with the loneliness thing going on, I'm thinking that my judgment may not be too good, and he was sounding like maybe he was wanting to *make up* for the other night.

(She smiles mischievously.)

So, I say no. It's not a good time. And we leave it there. Monday morning I flew to Cincinnati and made my presentation and it went over like gangbusters. Very successful. My boss says, "Michelle, go home and get some sleep." Tuesday, I fly back, I get in and go on my computer of course, my only connection to the world, and Steve is on line so I instant message him and say, "Hey, you bum. What are you doing home from work?" And he wrote back, only it's not him. It's his friend and he tells me that Steve was killed in a car accident driving back from Las Vegas.

(She looks intently over the audience.)

MICHELLE. *(cont.)* Just like that. Gone. I told his friend who I was and that we had…Steve and I, gone out. Not like we knew each other very well or anything. And he tells me I can come to the funeral if I want. Well, the next few days were weird. I don't really remember the order of things or anything but I started sensing Steve around me.

(She reacts as if he is in close proximity.)

I could feel him somehow in my chest. My heart, maybe. I'm having pie at this restaurant with my girl-friend and I decided to try to explain to her…

(beat)

Right, I know. She's gonna think I'm nuts, right? Well, she didn't. She says that maybe the guy wants to tell me something. She says that maybe if I let him say what he wants to say, he'll leave me alone, 'cause it's a sort of sad feeling – this feeling in my chest – sad and heavy. So, right there in the restaurant, we flip this paper-placemat-thing over and I wrote out what seemed to be a letter, to his mom, from Steve. It basically just said that he loved her and that he was sorry and it all hap-pened so fast. And even though he's a little mixed up still, not to worry about him, that he's with Aunt Ellen and he's okay.

(beat)

MICHELLE. *(cont.)* I thought maybe I should send it to her, you know? Get the letter to his mom so I call his friend and I read him the letter and he tells Steve's mom and she said to send it – the letter. So, I guess it was what she needed to hear. So I guess that was good. It was all sort of a relief, really.

(beat)

MICHELLE. *(cont.)* I'm back in with my therapist and I'm talking to him about something or other, and suddenly I feel Steve back in the room…

(She reacts as if he is in close proximity.)

…in my chest, this amazingly deep sadness and I see this vehicle…

(She recalls seeing it, in her mind's eye.)

…his SUV rolling over and over and over and I feel all this confusion and…

(She shakes her head and stops.)

Anyway, instead of ignoring it and trying to continue on with my session, with my so-called "life," I decide to take a chance and tell my therapist what's going on. You know, be honest. He listens, of course and says, after two years of not talking, he says, "Tell him to go away." I looked at my therapist and I said, "Can I do that? He's like a ghost or something. Can I really just tell him to go away?" And he said, "Yes, you can."

(beat)

So, I did. And he left. And the pain left. No more sadness. No more tumbling cars. And I've been telling things that hurt to leave ever since.

(blackout)

IT'S THE SIMPLE THINGS

(AT RISE: **CHRIS,** *a man in his forties, enters from the changing room wearing only a paper-thin hospital robe tied in the back and matching slippers. He carries a see-through, plastic bag that contains his clothes, wallet and keys. There is a row of chairs upstage left but otherwise, the stage is empty.)*

CHRIS. *(crosses downstage center and addresses an unseen nurse)* Uhm. Excuse me, ma'am?

(beat)

Excuse me?

(beat)

I know you have a lot of paper work there but is there any way I could…? I mean, is this right? Did I do this right? They told me to put this thing on with the ties in the back, but as you can see, it's sort of forming a gaping hole back there and it's making me a little nuts.

(beat)

Little nuts.

(He shakes his head.)

Sorry. I didn't mean *little* nuts. There not little. They're precious, actually. Very precious to me.

(beat)

I mean…this can't be right, is it? Because, well…

(becoming indignant)

I wasn't raised like this. So I was thinking maybe I could turn it around the *other* way so I can tie it up securely and no one will have to be embarrassed. Em-BARE-ASSED.

(He shakes his head.)

CHRIS. *(cont.)* Sorry. I don't see how it could make that much difference if I just spun it around.

(no response)

Oh, sure, yeah. I can see you're busy. I'll just wait here, till you're…

(He sits on one of the cold chairs and when his naked fanny touches its surface, he jumps back up again and quickly crosses to the nurse.)

Listen. I got an idea. How 'bout I just put my underwear back on? Okay? Would that work? I'm having surgery today and I'm losing some *very* important parts, parts I've had for a *very* long time, so I was thinking it would be preferable if I didn't lose my dignity in the process.

(Receiving no response, **CHRIS** *takes his underwear out of the plastic bag.)*

Well, okay. I'll just do that then.

(He crosses to same changing room, opens the door, then quickly closes it. He then addresses the person who was in the room.)

Oh, excuse me. Sorry. Sorry, I didn't know anyone had… You see, I was in there before you – changing. Never mind.

(He crosses away then turns back and reopens changing room door.)

You look much better in that than I do.

(He closes door and steps away. To self)

Maybe I got a woman's size by mistake.

(He crosses back to address the unseen nurse, downstage center.)

Hey listen, some other poor, unsuspecting fool has hijacked my changing room and I now have nowhere to change.

(no response)

CHRIS. *(cont.)* Right.

(He looks around very carefully, to self.)

Maybe I can just slip these back on while no one is…

(He removes his underwear from the plastic bag and seriously considers slipping them back on right there but feels too self-conscious. He crosses behind the row of chairs, lies down behind them and manages to pull the underwear back into place without any significant reveal. He sits up and then looks around.)

Jeez, no one's even looking. No one even sees me.

(He gets up.)

This is a very strange feeling. Am I…even here?

(He rushes downstage center, to nurse.)

Ma'am, I know you're very busy but I've got to know the truth – I haven't died, have I? Please tell me I'm not floating above this room somewhere while the surgeons are working on me below trying to revive me from some massive coronary I had while cut open on the operating table. We haven't even gone into surgery yet, right? I mean, I'm here.

(He slaps himself.)

I'm alive, right? Just answer this one question and I'll leave you alone.

(He nods along with her.)

A nod. Thank you. Thank you. I never knew a nod could mean so much to me. I really appreciate that. I really do. Thank you.

(He calms himself down by taking a deep breath, then retrieves a chair and brings it downstage center and sits.)

"It's the simple things." That's what my wife always says, "Honey, it's the simple things." And I said to her, "Then you have the operation." But you know, you can't argue with someone who's done all the research. You can't argue with someone like that and my wife always does *all* the research. "It's easier for the man," she says. "It's easier for the man to have the surgery – faster recovery time, less work missed, fewer complications." How can you argue with that? I can't argue with the truth. When she first "broached" the subject with me, I told her no. I won't do it. And she said, "You don't have the surgery, we don't have any more sex." And I thought, "Hell, it's better to be cut off than cut on…" But as you can see… I've changed my mind about that.

(vulnerably confessing)

CHRIS. *(cont.)* It's just that coming right down to it, it's hard, you know? When the rubber meets the road, it's…hard.

(beat)

Well, not hard, hard. I didn't mean…

(a quick look down)

…that. There's nothing hard about *that.*

(Due to paranoia, not reason, he leans in.)

I just need some reassurance, nurse. They don't cut them off, right? I mean, they don't actually…cut them off?

(blackout)

THE FREEWHEELIN' BOB DYLAN

(AT RISE: **JOEY**, *a man in his late 50's, visibly disabled, sits center stage. Next to him is an LP record-carrying trunk. He addresses the audience.)*

JOEY. My older brother, Dan, and I have collected records since…I don't know when – since we were kids. LP's, you know – Bob Dylan, Neil Young, The Doors… We loved the music and we both had quite an extensive collection. Some of them pretty valuable.

(beat)

When I was growing up, I used to keep them in a foot-locker, locked up. At the foot of my bed. Now I just keep them in here.

(He refers to the record-carrying trunk.)

I used to do this thing that would drive my brother crazy. When a new album was about to be released, I'd go and wait in line at the record store. You know, stand there till they opened. I had the patience. *I* was the one with the patience.

(beat)

Once I got inside, I wouldn't buy just one, I'd buy two – two copies of the same record. I'd leave one record sealed and open the other one so I could listen to it. Dylan was my favorite. I'd have the whole thing memorized within a couple of days or so.

(beat)

Well, I think I just got lucky or something 'cause one day, May, 1963… I was in eighth grade. I wait in line at the same ol' record store and I buy two copies of, "The Freewheelin' Bob Dylan" album on the Columbia label. Two copies.

(beat)

JOEY. *(cont.)* Unbelievable.

(beat)

Now, this record was actually released in a ton of different variations. There are copies that look exactly like the standard release, but play the withdrawn tracks. There are copies that list the withdrawn tracks but play the replacement tracks.

(beat)

It's confusing, I know. But take my word, to stumble onto this is unbelievable.

(He smiles.)

I bought two copies. Number CS-8786 in stereo. Stereo. It's got "360 sound stereo" in black on the label, *not white,* and it has no arrows. You know – the little arrows on either side of the "360 sound stereo?"

(beat)

They're not there. But this is what makes this particular LP extra, extra special. It has the withdrawn tracks listed on the sleeve, the label AND the record *plays them* – the songs – the withdrawn tracks – "Let Me Die in my Footsteps," "Rocks and Gravel," "Talkin' John Birch Blues" and "Gambling Willie's Dead Man's Hand." Not the standard release songs that the rest of the world heard when they listened to this album. We're talking rare. Rare.

(beat)

This album now books for over $30,000 in *near mint* condition and I had two – one sealed and one I'd listened to but was still pretty much mint. No known stereo copies play these songs and list them. And I had two copies. Who knows what the sealed one was worth.

(beat)

JOEY. *(cont.)* I've never really understood my brother. He was different from me. Just different. That's all I'm saying. We got along okay but I always knew inside, there was something different about him.

(beat)

1969, I get drafted into the army. Vietnam. It sucked. And I'm…sort of restricted now because of it. Can't work. I've lived with my parents ever since I got back because I can't work.

(beat)

1971, I come home, they sent me home 'cause I was done. Done. And I go to open my trunk and the sealed, "Freewheelin'" record is missing. I asked my mom if anyone had been in the trunk while I was gone and she swore no one had touched it. I had the only key and I took it with me to 'Nam. No one knew I had that record but my family and no one knew of its value except my older brother. Dan.

(beat)

Spending two years killing people with piano wire pretty much put me in a mood to confront, you know what I mean? Piano wire. I specialized in it.

(beat)

I drop by his house, without calling, and ask him about the record. Of course he denies it so I drop it. Believe it or not, I drop it. Mostly because he seemed to be telling the truth. But that's the difference between him and me. If I was lying, I couldn't look you in the face. He had no problem with this. No problem with lying and looking you right in the face. Well, I say to him, "Hey, if you don't have it, then you won't have any problem with me looking through your LP's." And he says to me, "I gave 'em to the Goodwill. Don't have any left. All gone, Joey. They're all gone." He looks me right in the eye and tells me this. I let it go.

(beat)

JOEY. *(cont.)* Well, after the funeral last week, I go over to the house. His wife asked me to. I go over there and she presents me with this box, this heavy box and they help me load it into my van. I get home, pull it out and it's all his old records.

(sarcastically)

The ones he gave to the Goodwill, I guess. Most of them beat up, you know, 'cause he didn't take care of 'em, but there's this one – sealed, mint. "Freewheelin' with Bob Dylan." "Freewheelin' with Bob Dylan!" Ain't no one had that sealed record in the world but me. No one but me. Can you imagine? The motherfucker stole it from me. His crippled brother. Just back from Vietnam. Can't work. Lyin' and lookin' me right in the eye. I call up his wife and she says, "Joey, go buy yourself a house. Go buy yourself a house." So I did. I fuckin' did, motherfucker.

(blackout)

CAUGHT IN A LIE

*(AT RISE: **MIRANDA**, a married woman of any age, sits center stage in a chair that faces stage right. She is holding a clipboard and pen and filling out medical forms, with her purse beside her. She turns to her left to address the audience.)*

MIRANDA. I bring my own clipboard. I mean, if you think about it, only sick people hold these things, you know? And *I* don't come to the doctor sick. I come to prevent sickness. So I don't want to be catching some strange disease from some ol' clipboard just because I have to sit here and fill out these stupid forms. Dear God. I mean, wouldn't that be ironic – come to the doctor to prevent sickness and I get sick.

(She returns to her writing, then stops.)

I use my own pens too.

(flicking it in the air)

Always my own pens. They offer them to you but I just say, "No." Some people chew on their pens and I don't like holding something, anything that's been chewed on. Dear God.

(beat)

I saw a pen once that looked like a pit bull had gotten hold of it. A pit bull! 'Course it wasn't a pit bull. It was my husband. He likes to stick foreign objects into his mouth – pens, Popsicle sticks, toothpicks, suckers… He tries to use normal-looking things when he's out in public. You know, so people won't catch on. Things you would expect to find in a person's mouth. But at home…

(She shakes her head.)

MIRANDA. *(cont.)* You should see our television remote. People think we have a pit bull. They think that because that's what I tell them, "We have a pit bull. Chews on everything in sight." I lie. I admit it. Who wouldn't, under these circumstances?

(She turns to face front.)

We had the Chalmers over for dinner a couple weeks ago and I forgot to put away all the chewed-up kitchen utensils that I still manage to squeeze some use out of. We were having pasta and…I don't know how I missed it but the ladle I used to serve the sauce…

(shudders at the memory)

Well, I'm sure you've got the idea.

(beat)

I had to come up with something. So I casually mentioned that we had a pit bull. And much to my dismay, they got all excited about that and wanted to see them. Two. Yes, I believe I said two pit bulls. Which is a bigger lie than just saying one, I suppose. And I didn't want to get caught in a lie. Dear God. I mean, who wants to get caught in a lie?!

(beat)

So, I tell them that "Chewy" and "Chewette" were at the vets for the night, getting their teeth scrubbed. My husband gives me this look. Like this was all somehow *my* fault. You know, this lying business.

(beat)

Well, we like the Chalmers. I mean, what's not to like? They're very clean people. She manages the bakery at Gelson's. You gotta be clean and sanitary to manage the bakery at Gelson's.

(beat)

MIRANDA. *(cont.)* They had us over to their house for dinner. We met their dogs. Very clean. Sanitary. So…I had to come up with something. My husband wouldn't go for actually getting pit bulls and to tell you the truth, by the looks of them, they're pigs – slobbering and making disgusting noises constantly. So, Saturday morning I took my husband's tape recorder over to the Pound. They always have a ton of pit bulls there. They lent me a clean chair and I sat by a couple of these dogs and recorded about three hours worth of… Pit Bull sounds. You know, slobbering and stuff. That's about how long a dinner party lasts with the Chalmers – three hours.

(beat)

They were over that night. Last Saturday and uhh…no glitches. Just ran the tape out in the garage. 'Course they wanted to *see* them – our dogs back from the vet with fresh, clean pearly whites but I explained to them that they were highly dangerous. You know, trained to kill on sight and the subject was quickly changed by my husband who was nervously chewing on the nearest electrical cord at the time. Not paying much attention to what he was doing. Next thing you know, poof, he's out like a light. Out cold. I thought he was dead at first. But Mr. Chalmers is a paramedic and pounded on his chest. He's fine now and that seemed to fix him of the habit. Now if I could just stop lying. It's so much fun.

(blackout)

End of Play

COSTUME PLOT

The Shoe Fetish
A simple, flowery blouse with matching slacks or skirt

The Kind That Doesn't Budge
Khaki pants with plaid, button-down shirt

The Eyes of a Mother
Earth-toned printed, long-sleeved blouse with matching slacks

Plaids and Stripes
Blue and white checkered, button-down shirt with yellow and white striped pants that do not match

The Quilt Maker
Billowy blouse with draw string, along with loose-fitting pants

The Dental Hygienist
Blue mechanic's button-down shirt, blue jeans, baseball cap and work boots

Shuffleboard
Gray khaki pants with a long-sleeved soft shirt and tennis shoes

Sensitivity
An elegant dress with t-strap shoes and a delicate necklace

It's the Simple Things
A blue, paper-thin hospital robe with matching paper-thin slippers

The Freewheelin' Bob Dylan
Short-sleeved, white t-shirt and blue jeans

Caught in a Lie
A sleeveless, upscale tank top with matching slacks

FURNITURE AND PROPERTY PLOT

The Shoe Fetish
> FURNITURE
> Small table, preset against stage right wall
> Small trunk, preset against upstage center wall
> A ramp, located downstage center that brings the lip of the stage gradually down to meet the floor on the audience level, allowing actors to enter the stage through the house
> HAND PROPS
> Shoe organizer, containing twelve pairs of shoes, hangs on upstage wall, stage left

The Kind That Doesn't Budge
> FURNITURE
> Chair, center stage

The Eyes of a Mother
> FURNITURE
> Small table, center stage
> PERSONAL PROPS
> A shallow bowl, so the act of cabbage-chopping can be seen
> Cabbage
> Cabbage chopper with stainless steel round-edged blade
> Tray able to contain all the above

The Quilt Maker
> FURNITURE
> Chair, center stage
> PERSONAL PROPS
> Eyeglasses connected to an eyeglass chain
> Hand-made quilt with said items somewhere present

The Dental Hygienist
> FURNITURE
> Chair, center stage, with the small table stage left of the chair
> PERSONAL PROPS
> Dixie cup containing Listerine, on table
> Round bowl containing water, on table
> Paper towel fastened with chain around actor's neck

Shuffleboard
> PERSONAL PROPS
> Three various winter coats on hangers, preset off-stage right

Sensitivity
> FURNITURE
> A stylish high stool with back support, center stage

It's the Simple Things
>FURNITURE
>A row of chairs upstage left
>PERSONAL PROPS
>A plastic, see-through bag that contains clothes, wallet and keys

The Freewheelin' Bob Dylan
>FURNITURE
>Wheelchair
>HAND PROPS
>An LP, record-carrying trunk

Caught in a Lie
>FURNITURE
>Chair, facing stage left
>PERSONAL PROPS
>Clipboard
>Pen
>Medical forms
>Purse

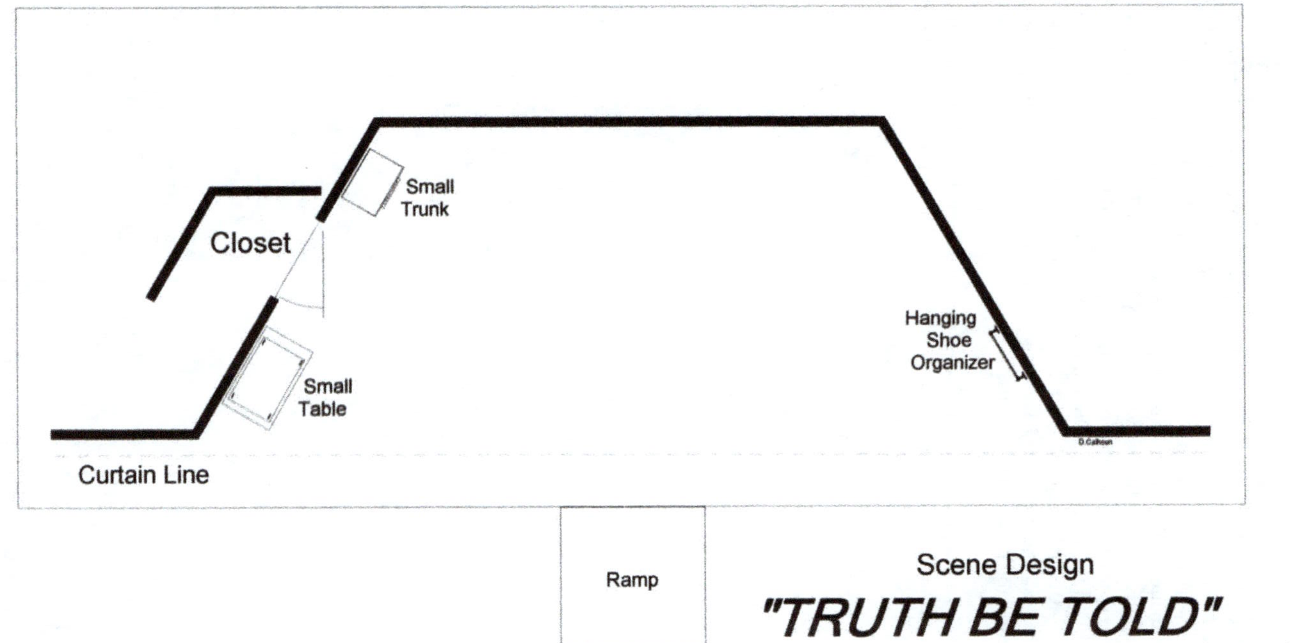

Closet
Small Trunk
Small Table
Hanging Shoe Organizer
D. Calhoun
Curtain Line
Ramp
Scene Design
"TRUTH BE TOLD"

ABOUT THE AUTHOR

LISA SOLAND's other Samuel French publications include *Waiting, Cabo San Lucas, The Name Game* and *The Man in the Gray Suit & Other Short Plays.* Her work can also be found in anthologies published by Applause Books, Dramatic Publishing and Smith and Kraus. From this collection, "The Kind that Doesn't Budge" was originally published in the premiere issue of *Quay* magazine (a journal of the arts) in May of 2007 and "The Freewheelin' Bob Dylan" was published in *Quay* magazine, Issue 2, Volume 2, in the July – December 2008 issue. She is a member of The Dramatists Guild of America, The Alliance of Los Angeles Playwrights and the International Centre for Women Playwrights.

Ms. Soland is the founder of The All Original Playwright Workshop, where she works as Artistic Director and teacher, producing workshops throughout the United States and online.